GLORY to the Father!

by Piera Paltro

Translated by
Daughters of St. Paul

Illustrated by
Anna Maria Curti

St. Paul Books & Media

Original Title: *Gloria*
© by Edizione Paoline 1978

ISBN 0-8198-3043-7

English edition, copyright © 1987 by the Daughters of St. Paul

Printed in the U.S.A., by St. Paul Books & Media
50 St. Paul's Ave., Boston, MA 02130

St. Paul Books & Media is the publishing house of the Daughters of St. Paul, an international congregation of women religious serving the Church with the communications media.

Glory...

I think that glory
is something for
emperors and generals,
when everyone
claps and shouts:
"Hooray!" because the emperors
and generals have done
something wonderful.

But, God,
You made the world...
and me in it...
and everyone else.
Surely You are
the most important
Person of all!

I bet that in Your House
everyone claps for You,
and gives You thanks,
because they know
that no one—but no one,
is like You.
No one knows
what You know.
No one can do everything,
and love everyone
like You do.

Many people forget this,
but I don't.
And I will always
think of You
when I say:

Glory

...to the Father, and to the Son, and to the Holy Spirit.

Jesus, when You came to earth
You said that
Your Father sent You,
and before You left us
You promised
that You would send
the Spirit.

So not only
You are God,
but the Father,
You and the Spirit, *all three*,
are the Living God.
To us You say:
"God is Love!
We Three are Love!"

I'm happy
that the Father is God.
I trust in Him.
I'm happy
that the Son is God.
He is Jesus, my brother.
I'm happy
that the Holy Spirit is God.
He always speaks to my heart.

When I go to church
I feel that everyone
is happy like me.
I can tell because
they always say
these three names together.
And so glory is for all three:

to the Father,
and to the Son,
and to the Holy Spirit...

as it was in the beginning

My teacher said that
before people
existed on earth
there were
already animals,
and even before that
there were plants,
and even before that
there were icebergs
and oceans,
and even before that,
when there wasn't
anything yet,
at the very beginning,
You, Who are Father
and Son and Spirit,
said: "How good it is!
Let us make the world!"

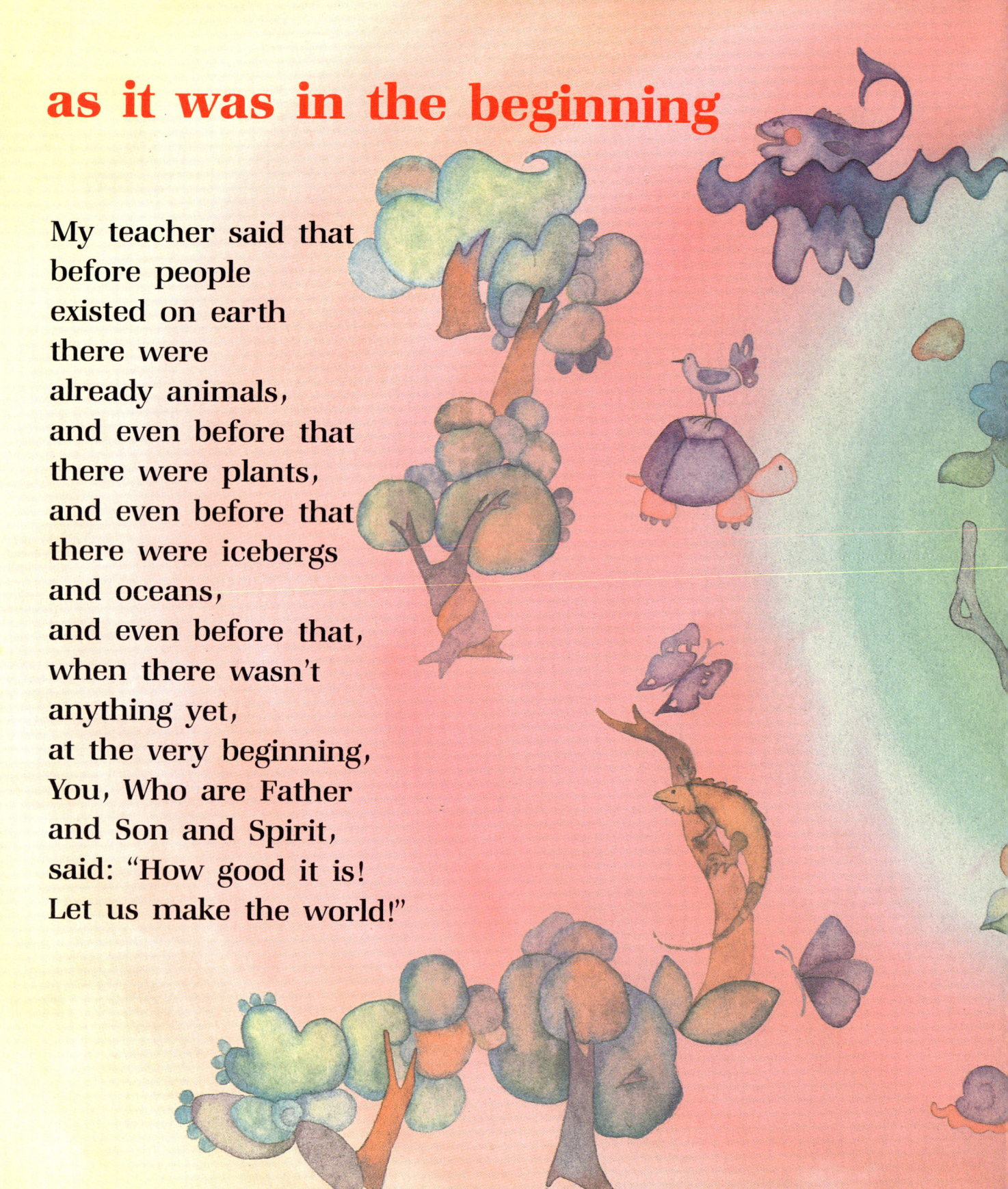

This is what it means to say
that *You existed from the beginning.*
When I get to heaven
I'm going to try to look back
to see where it all began.
You will laugh
and tell me:
"But I have always existed!"

...is now and will be forever

I'm not very big yet,
But I *am* growing—
everyone says so.
Someday I'll become a teenager,
then an adult,
like Dad.
Later,
even though it seems strange now,
I'll become a little old man.
If You give me
a hundred years,
I'll be a century old!
Then I will come to You
and I will see
that You don't need to grow
and You never grow old.

You're always Father,
and You are always Son
with the Father,
and You are always
Spirit of Love between
them both.
You're always happy
and always good,
and You have already
listened to the prayers
of many children
like me.
You never change!

You are a great mystery!
But that is OK.
I like
the way You are,
and when
I think of You
It makes me happy.
So I say:
Glory

**...now
  and
    forever**

Sometimes
(and not only when I'm scolded)
I feel like going
on a rocket to the sky,
higher and higher,
without ever stopping.
Where would I end up?

If I traveled
thousands of years
or one million years
or thousands of millions...
Wow!
When I arrived back on earth
I wouldn't find anyone!

And if after a trip like that
I landed back in our country
and found that everything
had become like it is
on the moon...
where there is
no air, or water,
or anything...
what a surprise that would be!

But even then
I would hear Your voice
telling me:
"Hello!
Ten million centuries
have passed by,
but I am here.
I am the Father, the Son and the Spirit.
I am God and I have been waiting for you."
I wouldn't be afraid then.
Yes, God,
it's wonderful
that You live **forever and ever**

Amen.

Yes, I say *Amen.*
Amen means
"I agree."
And I
really mean it
when I say
I would not want
to have any other God
than You—
Father and Son and Holy Spirit.
Whenever I think of You
I say
in my heart
or out loud:

...Glory to
the Father,
and to the Son,
and to the Holy Spirit:
as it was
in the beginning,
is now,
and will be forever.
Amen.

VISIT, WRITE or CALL your nearest ST. PAUL BOOK & MEDIA CENTER today for a wide selection of Catholic books, periodicals, cassettes, quality video cassettes for children and adults! Operated by the Daughters of St. Paul.

We are located in:

ALASKA
   750 West 5th Ave., Anchorage, AK 99501 907-272-8183.
CALIFORNIA
   3908 Sepulveda Blvd., Culver City, CA 90230 310-397-8676.
   1570 Fifth Ave. (at Cedar Street), San Diego, CA 92101 619-232-1442
   46 Geary Street, San Francisco, CA 94108 415-781-5180.
FLORIDA
   145 S.W. 107th Ave., Miami, FL 33174 305-559-6715; 305-559-6716.
HAWAII
   1143 Bishop Street, Honolulu, HI 96813 808-521-2731.
ILLINOIS
   172 North Michigan Ave., Chicago, IL 60601 312-346-4228; 312-346-3240.
LOUISIANA
   4403 Veterans Memorial Blvd., Metairie, LA 70006 504-887-7631; 504-887-0113.
MASSACHUSETTS
   50 St. Paul's Ave., Jamaica Plain, Boston, MA 02130 617-522-8911.
   Rte. 1, 885 Providence Hwy., Dedham, MA 02026 617-326-5385.
MISSOURI
   9804 Watson Rd., St. Louis, MO 63126 314-965-3512; 314-965-3571.
NEW JERSEY
   561 U.S. Route 1, Wick Plaza, Edison, NJ 08817 908-572-1200.
NEW YORK
   150 East 52nd Street, New York, NY 10022 212-754-1110.
   78 Fort Place, Staten Island, NY 10301 718-447-5071; 718-447-5086.
OHIO
   2105 Ontario Street (at Prospect Ave.), Cleveland, OH 44115 216-621-9427.
PENNSYLVANIA
   214 W. DeKalb Pike, King of Prussia, PA 19406 215-337-1882; 215-337-2077.
SOUTH CAROLINA
   243 King Street, Charleston, SC 29401 803-577-0175.
TEXAS
   114 Main Plaza, San Antonio, TX 78205 512-224-8101.
VIRGINIA
   1025 King Street, Alexandria, VA 22314 703-549-3806.
CANADA
   3022 Dufferin Street, Toronto, Ontario, Canada M6B 3T5 416-781-9131.